This book belongs to
_____

Nicholas
_____

From
Grandma
Dalbis

Goldilocks and the Three Bears

BARRON'S
New York. Toronto

Once upon a time there was a young girl named Goldilocks. She was called Goldilocks because of her long, golden hair.

One day, while walking in the forest, she came upon a small cottage. Something in the kitchen smelled delicious, and as she was very hungry, she went inside to see what smelled so good.

In the kitchen, she found three bowls of porridge on a wooden table. She took a small taste from the big bowl. It was too hot. Next she tried some from the medium-sized bowl, but it was too cold. Last of all, she tasted some from the teeny-tiny bowl—and it was just right! She ate a little more…and then just a bit more, until soon she had finished the whole bowl.

Since she was a curious girl, she decided to look around the cottage. She went into the living room, where she found three wooden chairs. First she tried the big chair, but it was too high. Then she tried the medium-sized chair, but it was't much better. Finally, she sat on the teeny-tiny chair and found that it was just right. But all of a sudden, the chair broke and she fell down.

Goldilocks soon forgot all about the chair because she was feeling sleepy. She looked around for a place to take a nap. She went upstairs and found a bedroom with three beds. She climbed into the great big bed, but it was too hard. Next she tried the medium-sized bed, but it was too soft. Then she got into the teeny-tiny bed and discovered that it was just right. She soon fell fast asleep.

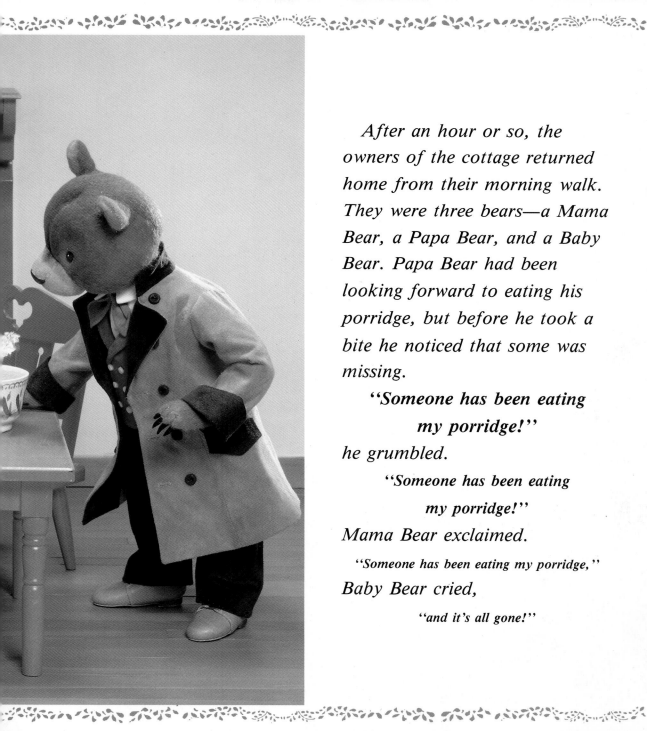

After an hour or so, the owners of the cottage returned home from their morning walk. They were three bears—a Mama Bear, a Papa Bear, and a Baby Bear. Papa Bear had been looking forward to eating his porridge, but before he took a bite he noticed that some was missing.

**"Someone has been eating
my porridge!"**
he grumbled.

**"Someone has been eating
my porridge!"**
Mama Bear exclaimed.

"Someone has been eating my porridge,"
Baby Bear cried,

"and it's all gone!"

The Three Bears went into the
living room. Papa Bear growled,
**"Someone has been sitting
in my chair!"**
And Mama Bear said,
**"Someone has been sitting
in my chair, too!"**
Then Baby Bear yelped,
**"Someone has been sitting in my chair—and
now it's all broken!"**
With that, he began to cry.

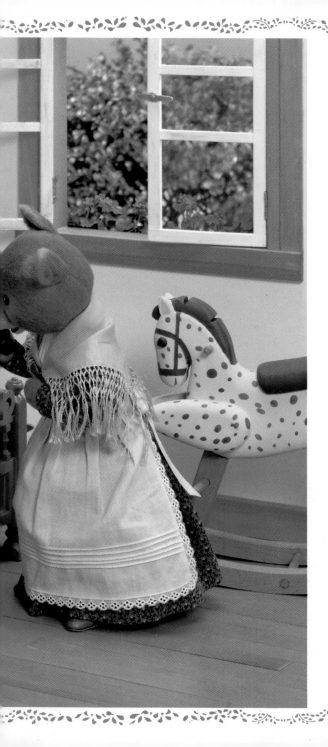

Then the Three Bears went upstairs and into their bedroom. Papa Bear said in his deep voice,

"Someone has been sleeping in my bed!"

And Mama Bear cried,

"Someone has been sleeping in my bed, too!"

But Baby Bear squealed,

"Someone has been sleeping in my bed— and she's still in it!"

Their cries woke up Goldilocks, who, of course, was frightened to see three bears.

Goldilocks jumped up and ran out of the cottage as fast as she could.

She never again went into anyone else's house uninvited.